To Lois, my wonderful sister — S.M.

To my wonderful wife, P.J. — J.L.

Library of Congress Cataloging-in-Publication Data

Metzger, Steve.
Pluto visits Earth! / by Steve Metzger ; illustrated by Jared Lee. — 1st ed.
p. cm.
Summary: Angry at being downgraded to a dwarf planet by Earth scientists, Pluto travels through the solar
system, asking other planets along the way for support, in hopes of regaining his planetary status.
ISBN 978-0-545-24934-8
[1. Pluto (Dwarf planet)—Fiction. 2. Solar system—Fiction.] I. Lee, Jared D., ill. II. Title.
PZ7.M56775Plu 2012
[E]—dc23
                                                2011026813
10 9 8 7 6 5 4 3 2 1   12 13 14 15 16

Printed in Singapore 46
First edition, August 2012

The display type was set in HouseHolidayPS.
The text was set in Bramley.
The art was created using a Rapidograph pen and Luma dyes on 4-ply Strathmore bristol (vellum) paper.
Book design by Whitney Lyle and Cindy Lin

Pluto
Visits Earth!

By **Steve Metzger**
Illustrated by **Jared Lee**

Orchard Books | New York
An Imprint of Scholastic Inc.

It was a quiet day in the universe when Pluto got the news.

"Hey, Pluto!" shouted Speedy the space rock, who was racing by with his friends. "You're not a planet anymore!"

"What are you talking about?" Pluto asked.

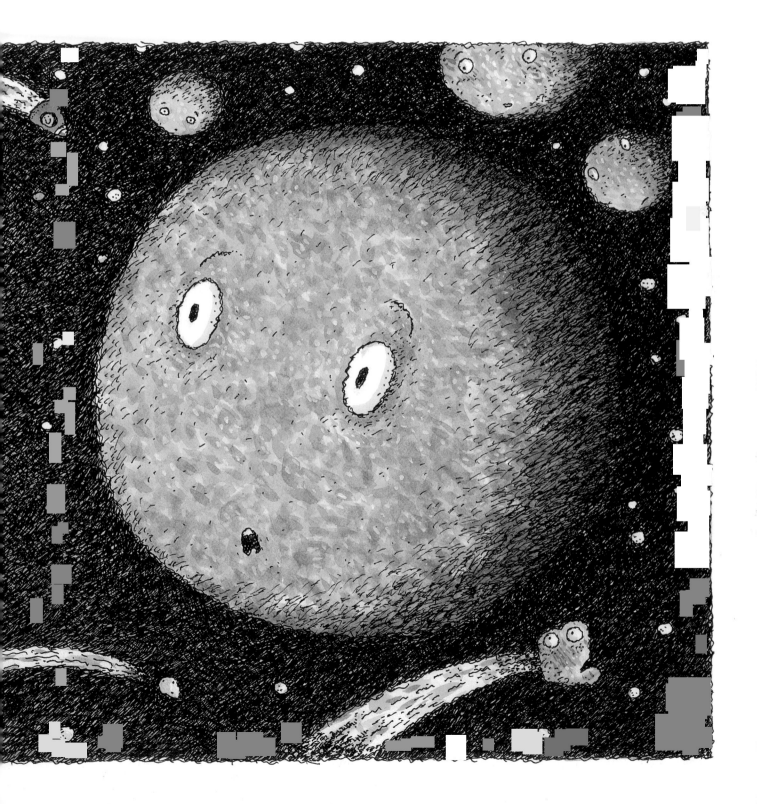

"Astronomers on Earth say you're a dwarf planet, not a real planet."

"A dwarf planet?" Pluto shouted out. "Wait a minute! Tell me more!"

"That's the way the comet crumbles," Speedy said.

Pluto turned purple with rage.

"How can this be?" he shouted. "I'm madder than a Martian!"

Pluto called out to his three moons. "Do I look small?"

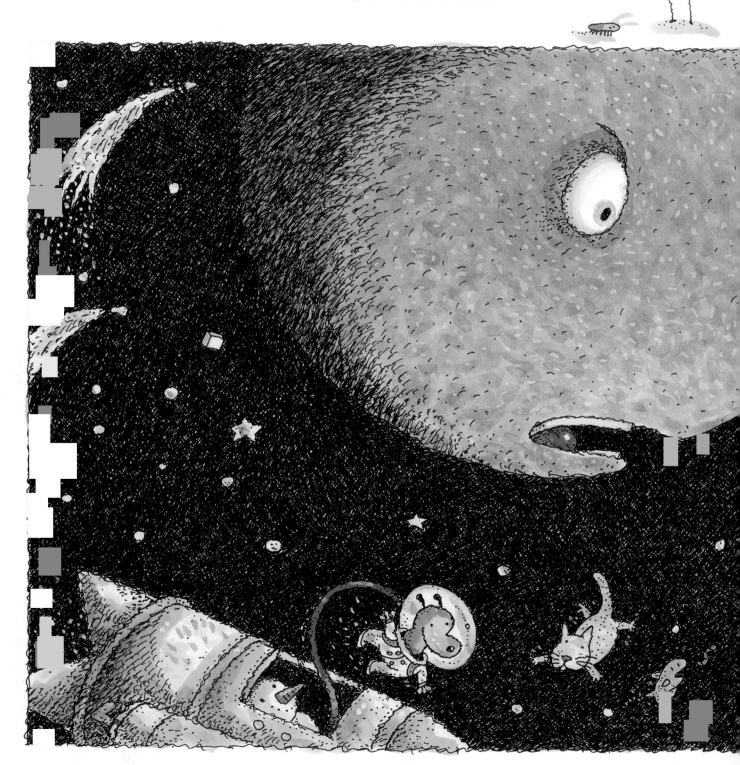

"Not to me, big guy!" Nix said.

"Well, you're twice as big as I am," Charon added.

Pluto thought, *I remember when I was named by Venetia Burney, that nice English girl.*

"But now this!" he yelled. "A dwarf planet! Hmpff! I'll go visit Earth and demand to be a real planet again!"

And with a mighty thrust, Pluto left his orbit and zoomed toward Earth. He asked other planets to help him out along the way.

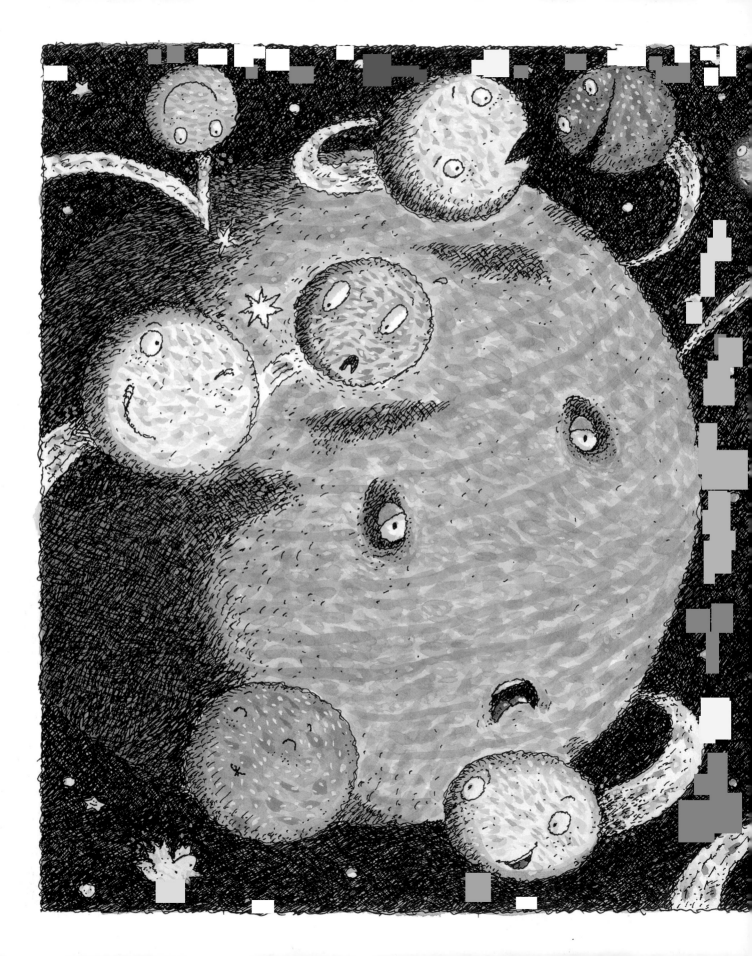

He saw Neptune in the distance.

"Halt! Who goes there?" Neptune shouted. "Friend or UFO?"

"It's me — Pluto!"

"Hi, little buddy," Neptune boomed. "Hey, I heard the big news. That's too bad. What brings you here?"

"I'm on my way to Earth," Pluto replied. "I want to be a regular planet again. Will you join me?"

"Sorry, Pluto," Neptune said. "I'd love to, but I've got thirteen moons to look after. I'm just too busy."

The other planets were no help, either.

Uranus was too scared.

Saturn was too vain.

Jupiter was too bossy.

Mars was too distracted.

Pluto didn't even bother visiting Venus and Mercury.

They were out of his way.

Pluto put on the brakes at the Mount Baldy Observatory and hovered above the astronomers. Two of them stepped forward.

"Why did you make me a dwarf planet?" Pluto thundered. The astronomers trembled.

"First of all, Mr. Pluto," Astronomer A said in a shaky voice, "you are small — much smaller than the other eight planets."

"So what?" Pluto answered. "I've still got a big heart!"

"Planets should be much larger than their moons," Astronomer B added. "You're not."

"I don't care!" Pluto said. "I liked being one of the nine planets in the solar system. Now nobody will know who I am."

"Excuse me," a boy shouted. "I have something to say."

The astronomers stepped back.

"Pluto, you will always be my favorite," the child said.

"I will?" Pluto said.

"Small or big, it doesn't matter," the child said. "You're the best!"

Pluto spun around. "Well, what do you think of that? I'm special!" He looked toward the sun. "I'd better get going. It's so hot here that I'm starting to melt."

As Pluto zoomed away, he shouted. "Good-bye, Earth. See you around the Milky Way!"

Pluto was discovered in 1930 by Clyde Tombaugh, an astronomer with the Lowell Observatory in Flagstaff, Arizona. It became the ninth planet in the solar system, the farthest from the sun. The other planets that orbit the sun are Mercury, Venus, Earth, Mars, Jupiter, Saturn, Uranus, and Neptune. Pluto's name was suggested by Venetia Burney, an eleven-year-old girl from Oxford, England.

Pluto is composed primarily of rock and ice. It has three moons: Charon, Nix, and Hydra. Pluto is relatively small, approximately one-third the size of Earth's moon and only twice as large as its own moon Charon.

In August 2006, the members of the International Astronomical Union decided that Pluto did not meet all of the requirements to be a planet. In addition to orbiting the sun (which Pluto does) and having a spherical shape (which Pluto has), a planet needs to use its gravity to clear its orbit of any asteriods (which Pluto does not). For this reason, the astronomers reclassified Pluto as a dwarf planet.

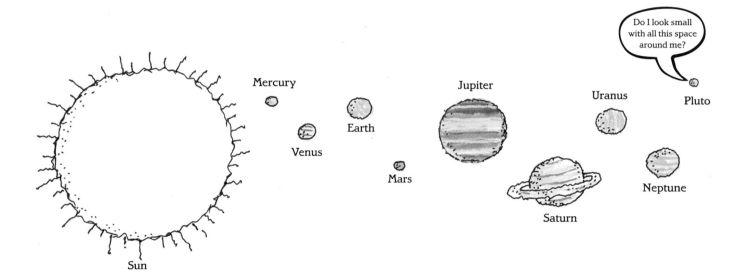